This edition is published by Armadillo,
an imprint of Anness Publishing Ltd, Blaby Road,
Wigston, Leicestershire LE18 4SE; info@anness.com

www.annesspublishing.com

If you like the images in this book and would like to investigate using
them for publishing, promotions or advertising, please visit our website
www.practicalpictures.com for more information.

A CIP catalogue record for this book is available from the British Library.

Publisher: Joanna Lorenz
Editorial Consultant: Jackie Fortey
Project Editors: Belinda Wilkinson and Richard McGinlay
Production Controller: Steve Lang

PUBLISHER'S NOTE
The author and publishers have made every effort to ensure that this book
is safe for its intended use, and cannot accept any legal responsibility
or liability for any harm or injury arising from misuse.

Manufacturer: Anness Publishing Ltd,
Blaby Road, Wigston, Leicestershire LE18 4SE, England
For Product Tracking go to: www.annesspublishing.com/tracking
Batch: 1017-22580-1127

A Storyteller Book

The Jungle Book

by Rudyard Kipling

Retold by Lesley Young
Illustrated by Jenny Thorne

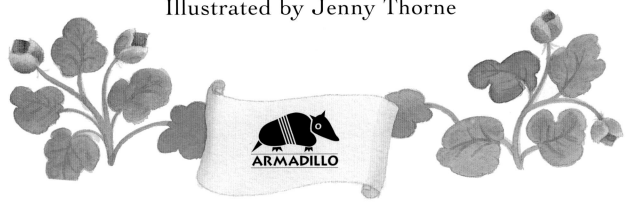

ARMADILLO

In a cave deep in the Indian jungle, a wolf woke up from his day's rest, yawned and stretched himself. The moon shone in at the mouth of the cave, where Mother Wolf was lying, while their four cubs jumped all over her, squealing.

"Time to hunt again," said Father Wolf. He was just about to go out hunting when he was stopped in his tracks by a loud angry snarl, coming from far below in the valley.

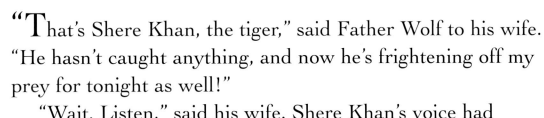

"That's Shere Khan, the tiger," said Father Wolf to his wife. "He hasn't caught anything, and now he's frightening off my prey for tonight as well!"

"Wait. Listen," said his wife. Shere Khan's voice had changed into a humming purr that filled the heavy jungle air.

"He's not hunting bulls or bucks tonight," she went on, "That's the sound he makes when he's hunting man."

The noise grew louder, and ended in the deafening roar of the tiger charging, followed quickly by a painful howl.

"I know what's happened," said Father Wolf, "the stupid beast has jumped on a wood-cutter's camp fire, and burned his feet."

"Quiet! Something is coming up the hill," said Mother Wolf, twitching her ears.

Father Wolf went outside the cave and got ready to
spring at therustling bushes. He bounded high into the air, but
suddenly saw what he was leaping at, and stopped himself just
in time, landing with a soft thud back down in the same place.

"Look!" he cried, "A man-cub!"

Right in front of the cave, was a small brown boy, just old
enough to walk. He looked up into the wolf's face and laughed,
showing white teeth and dimples.

"I have never seen a man-cub," said Mother Wolf, "bring it here." Father Wolf's jaws closed over the boy's back, and he carried him into the cave as gently as if he were carrying an egg. He dropped the man-cub amongst his own litter, and immediately the boy was pushing the wolf cubs aside, to get to their mother's warm fur.

Suddenly the moonlight was blocked out of the cave as Shere Khan's huge head appeared just inside.

"My prey – a man-cub – came this way," roared the tiger. "Its parents have run off, and now I want it. Give it to me."

The wolves knew that Shere Khan could not squeeze into the narrow cave.

"The wolves are a free people," growled Father Wolf. "We take orders from the head of the pack, not from you."

The tiger's roar filled the cave with a noise like thunder, and the cubs sprang back in fright, but Mother Wolf patted the boy with her paw and snarled fearlessly at the tiger.

"The man-cub is mine! He will learn to live with the pack and hunt with the pack, and in the end he will hunt you, too, Shere Khan!"

The tiger knew better than to fight an angry mother and he backed out of the cave. As he slunk back downhill, he roared over his shoulder,

"The man-cub will end up between my teeth sooner or later."

"Will you really keep him?" asked Father Wolf, when Shere Khan had gone.

"He came here alone, naked and hungry, but he was not afraid," said Mother Wolf.

"Of course I will keep him. I will call him Mowgli, little frog, but we will have to take him to the next pack meeting."

On the night of the pack meeting, Akela, the big lone wolf who led the pack, lay stretched out on a huge rock. Below him in a circle sat about forty wolves of every size and shade.

Suddenly Mowgli was pushed into the middle of the circle by Father Wolf. He sat there, laughing and playing with some pebbles in the moonlight. Akela was looking down at him, and all the wolves waited to hear what he would say, when the muffled roar of Shere Khan came from behind the rocks:

"The cub is mine. Give him to me. What use have you for a man-cub?"

The law of the jungle laid down that, in order to join the wolf pack, a cub must be spoken for by at least two members of the pack who were not his mother and father.

"Who speaks for this cub?" barked Akela.

The only other creature allowed at the council was Baloo, a sleepy brown bear who taught the cubs the law of the jungle. He got up on his hindquarters and growled, "I will speak for the man-cub. Let him run with the pack, and I will teach him."

"We need one other voice," said Akela.

A dark shadow dropped down into the circle. It was Bagheera, the black panther, who was as cunning as a fox but had a voice as soft as wild honey.

"I know I have no right to be here," he purred, "but I will give you a bull I have just killed if you will accept the man-cub into the pack. It would be a shame to kill a cub as smooth and naked as that one – and it may be more fun to hunt it when it is grown."

The voices of lots of wolves rose in the night air:

"It will scorch in the summer sun, anyway. What harm can a naked frog do us?"

"Take him away," said Akela to Father Wolf, "and train him as a free pack member."

So Mowgli went home with his new wolf family, laughing all the way, and never guessing how close to danger he had come.

During the next ten summers Baloo taught Mowgli the law of the jungle. He showed him how to tell a rotten branch from a good one, and many other things.

"Speak politely to the wild bees, when you come across a hive," he told him, "and they might give you some honey."

"And always warn the water snakes before you splash down into one of their pools," he added.

One day, Bagheera, the black panther, was lying in the shade, watching Baloo teaching Mowgli.

"How can his little head carry all these things?" Bagheera asked the big bear.

"Is there anything in the jungle too little to be killed?" answered Baloo. "That's why he must learn."

Mowgli ran over and jumped on to Bagheera's back, pulling at his fur and chattering loudly,

"Don't worry, Bagheera. Some day soon I'm going to have a tribe of my own and lead them through the branches. And then we'll throw twigs and dirt down on old Baloo!"

"Wait a minute," said Baloo, scooping Mowgli off the panther's back with his huge paw, "you've been talking to the monkeys, those silly creatures who eat everything and don't have any laws."

"I was tired of learning all these rules," said Mowgli, "so I went off on my own and the monkeys came down from the trees and played with me."

"We jungle creatures don't have anything to do with the monkeys," said Baloo, as a shower of nuts and twigs rained down on their heads.

The monkeys were always meaning to get a leader, and have laws of their own. They never did because they couldn't remember anything from one day to the next. But they were very angry when they heard Baloo call them silly animals, not fit for Mowgli to play with.

"I've had an idea," screeched one monkey. "Let's capture the man-cub. He can show us how to build shelters – I've seen him weave sticks. We could make him our leader and all the other animals would be jealous."

The monkeys followed Baloo,
Bagheera and Mowgli through the
jungle very quietly until it was time
for their midday nap. Mowgli, who
had promised to have nothing more
to do with the monkeys, was
sleeping soundly between the black
panther and the bear. The next
thing he knew, Mowgli was
being pulled along by lots of
strong, hard little hands.
He looked back and saw
Baloo, up on his hind
legs, giving a huge
roar and waking up
the whole jungle.

The monkeys dragged Mowgli up a tree until he felt the thin, topmost branches bending beneath him. Then the monkeys, holding him tightly, flung themselves into mid-air and caught hold of the branches of the next tree with a great *Whoop*!

The monkeys were going so fast that Mowgli knew his friends would soon be left far behind. If he looked down, all he saw was a thick sea of branches. So he looked up, and there he saw Chil the hawk, balancing and wheeling on the wind as he flew over the jungle looking for prey.

Chil was amazed to see a man-cub
being rushed through the trees by the
monkeys. But he was even more
amazed when the little brown figure
shouted up a perfect hawk call, just
as Baloo had taught him.

"Mark my trail and tell Baloo and
Bagheera where I am," called Mowgli.

Meanwhile, Baloo and Bagheera
were panting after the monkeys.
Every now and then, Bagheera
would climb up a tree to try and
reach them.

However, the thin branches would not bear the panther's weight and he slithered back down, his claws full of bark.

At last he stopped and said, "What we need is a rescue plan. They may drop him if we follow too closely."

"You're right," said Baloo, "I know – we must find Kaa the rock snake. The monkeys are terrified of him because he can climb as well as they can, and he steals young monkeys in the night. The very mention of his name makes their tails go cold."

Baloo and Bagheera found Kaa stretched out on a warm ledge admiring his beautiful new coat. For the past ten days he had been out of action, changing his skin, and now he was feeling splendid and looking forward to dinner.

"Good hunting!" called Baloo.

"He!" hissed Kaa. "Don't speak to me about hunting. The branches are all dry and rotten, so I have to spend half a night climbing on the chance of catching one young monkey."

"Don't speak to me about monkeys."

"Yes, monkeys are so rude," said Bagheera. "To call a noble creature like yourself a footless, yellow earthworm . . ."

Kaa hissed again and the muscles in his throat tensed in anger.

"They called me thissss?"

Just then Chil the hawk swooped down and called to Baloo,

"I have a message for you from the man-cub. The monkeys have taken him to the monkey city."

"So, Mowgli remembered the hawk call even while he was being dragged through the trees," said Baloo proudly.

The three animals sped off to the monkey city. It was called the Cold Lairs, and was an old deserted city, built by man, but now buried deep in the jungle where few animals, apart from the monkeys, ever went.

In the Cold Lairs, the monkeys were very pleased with themselves and their new plaything. Mowgli looked around in amazement at the grand, crumbling buildings all covered with ivy. There was a great palace without a roof, and trees were growing through its walls.

"I'm hungry," said Mowgli at last. "Bring me food or let me hunt here – it is the law of the jungle."

Some monkeys bounded away to fetch him nuts and papayas, but they started squabbling together and completely forgot what they had set out to do.

Mowgli could do nothing but wait.

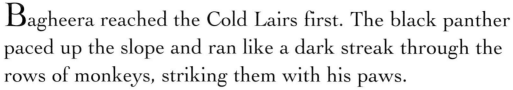

Bagheera reached the Cold Lairs first. The black panther paced up the slope and ran like a dark streak through the rows of monkeys, striking them with his paws.

"Hide the man-cub!" screeched a crowd of monkeys, grabbing Mowgli and dragging him towards an old summer house. They stood on each others' shoulders to make a pyramid, pulled Mowgli up and pushed him in through the broken roof.

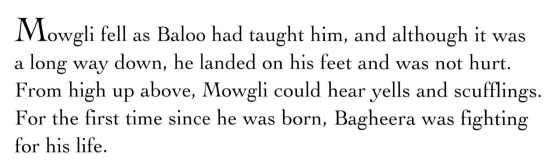

Mowgli fell as Baloo had taught him, and although it was a long way down, he landed on his feet and was not hurt. From high up above, Mowgli could hear yells and scufflings. For the first time since he was born, Bagheera was fighting for his life.

"Go to the water tank, Bagheera," shouted Mowgli, "the monkeys can't swim."

Mowgli's cry gave Bagheera new strength, and he began to work his way through the mass of monkeys to the tank. Suddenly a war cry rang out through the air. Baloo had arrived. He began to move through the monkeys, clearing a path with wide swipes of his paw.

Mowgli heard a huge splash, which told him that the panther had found the water, where the monkeys could not follow. But there were so many of them. Where was Kaa, the snake?

Bagheera lifted up his dripping chin and gave a snake call. Kaa had been slithering along as fast as he could, but he had only just reached the Cold Lairs. He raised his head and held his body up like a battering ram as he struck into the crowd of monkeys around Baloo.

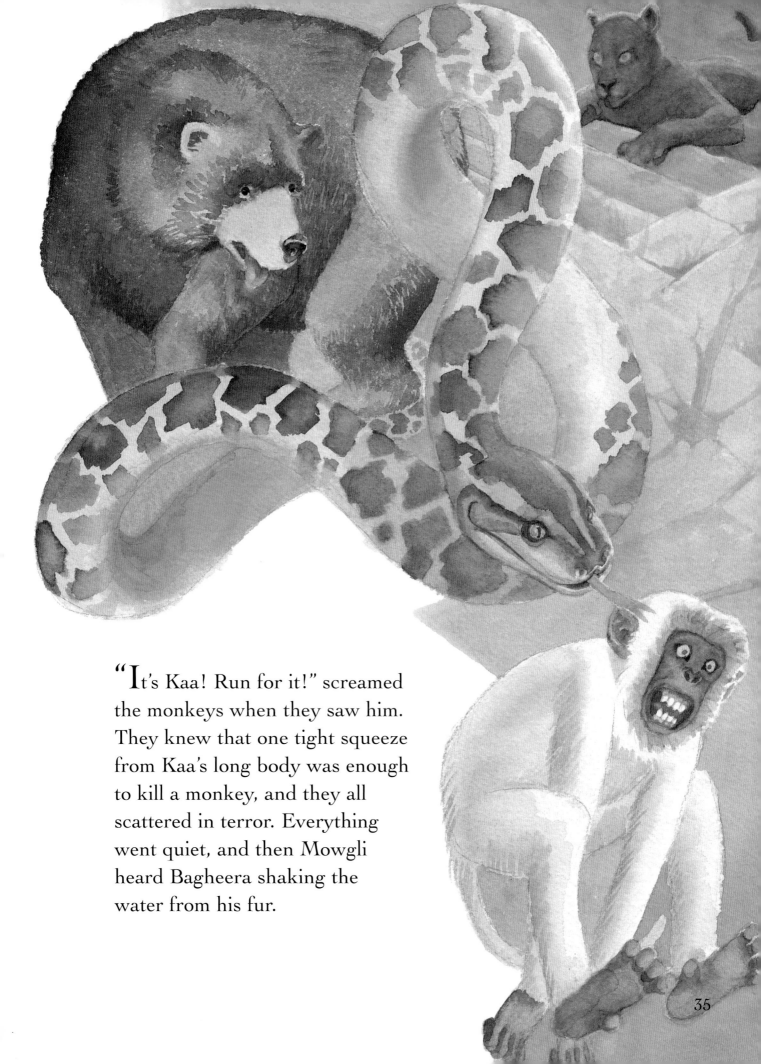

"It's Kaa! Run for it!" screamed
the monkeys when they saw him.
They knew that one tight squeeze
from Kaa's long body was enough
to kill a monkey, and they all
scattered in terror. Everything
went quiet, and then Mowgli
heard Bagheera shaking the
water from his fur.

"I'm in here," shouted Mowgli, and his friends followed the
sound of his voice to the old summer house. Kaa looked until he
saw a crack in the walls. Then he lifted his long body up clear
of the ground, and struck six blows at the bricks. The walls
broke and fell away in a cloud of dust, and Mowgli leapt out
and flung himself between Baloo and Bagheera, putting an arm
round each neck. Kaa looked him up and down.

"Be careful," hissed the snake, "that I don't mistake you for
a monkey, some dark night when I have just changed my skin."

The moon was now sinking behind the hills, and all the monkeys had gathered again and were huddled together along the old ruined walls.

Kaa coiled his body into a circle, swinging his head from side to side. Then he began making loops and figures of eight with his body, and humming a low, lazy song. Bagheera and Baloo were rooted to the spot. The monkeys swayed forward helplessly, and Bagheera and Baloo took another step forward with them.

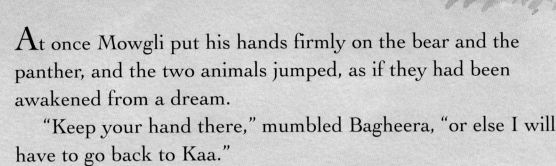

At once Mowgli put his hands firmly on the bear and the
panther, and the two animals jumped, as if they had been
awakened from a dream.

"Keep your hand there," mumbled Bagheera, "or else I will
have to go back to Kaa."

"Don't be silly," laughed Mowgli, "it's only old Kaa making
circles in the dust."

The man-cub, the panther and the bear slipped out through
a gap in the wall and back into the jungle.

When Mowgli had been in the jungle about ten years, Bagheera the panther said to him,

"Akela is very old and some day soon he will no longer be the leader of the pack. Many of the young wolves believe Shere Khan when he says that a man-cub has no place in a wolf pack."

"I was born in the jungle!" exclaimed Mowgli. "There is no wolf from whose paws I have not pulled a thorn."

"If you feel under my chin," purred Bagheera, "you will find a bald spot, rubbed by a collar. You see I, too, was born among men, and lived in a king's palace until I escaped. That's why I gave a bull for you at the pack council when you were just a tiny cub. Now you must go back to men or you will be killed in the jungle."

Bagheera looked kindly at young Mowgli,

"I think you are in danger already, but you can run down to the huts in the valley and take some of the red flower that the people there grow. That will be a stronger friend to you than either Baloo or me."

The red flower was fire. The animals all feared it so much, that they could not even call it by its proper name.

Mowgli ran down to the valley and pressed his face against the window of a hut. He saw a boy picking up a pot, which he filled with lumps of red-hot charcoal and took outside.

Mowgli strode over, took the pot from the boy and rushed off with it, leaving the boy howling with fear.

Mowgli blew into the pot and dropped twigs into it to keep the fire going as he carried it back up the hill.

That night, at the council meeting, Shere Khan the tiger began to speak.

"What right has he to speak," shouted Mowgli, "just because Akela is growing old? Tigers do not belong in our pack."

Shere Khan roared angrily:

"This man-cub was meant to be my dinner from the start. He has troubled the jungle for ten seasons, but what has a man to do with us?"

"A man! What has he to do with us?" yelled more than half the wolf pack.

Mowgli stood up and shouted at them, "I, the man, have brought a little of the red flower which you, dogs, fear."

He threw the pot of fire on the ground amongst some dead wood and the pack drew back in terror before the leaping flames. Mowgli picked up a branch, lit it in the flames and beat Shere Khan over the head with it until the tiger whimpered with fear.

"Go, singed jungle cat," shouted Mowgli, "and the next time I come to this rock it will be as a man – with your hide. "*Go!*"

Soon there was no-one left at the council rock except Mowgli, Akela, Bagheera and a few wolves. Suddenly something made Mowgli catch his breath, and hot tears ran down his cheeks.

"What are these?" he said, wiping his face, "Am I dying, Bagheera?"

"No, little brother," said the panther sadly, "but now I know you are a man, and not a cub. The jungle is no longer a safe home for you. They are only tears Mowgli, let them fall."

"I will go to men now," said Mowgli, "But first I must say goodbye to my mother."

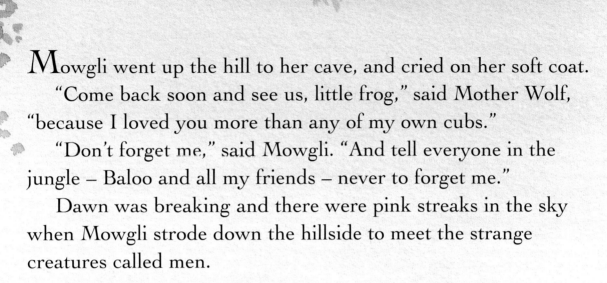

Mowgli went up the hill to her cave, and cried on her soft coat.

"Come back soon and see us, little frog," said Mother Wolf, "because I loved you more than any of my own cubs."

"Don't forget me," said Mowgli. "And tell everyone in the jungle – Baloo and all my friends – never to forget me."

Dawn was breaking and there were pink streaks in the sky when Mowgli strode down the hillside to meet the strange creatures called men.